KU-223-384

30131 05718887 9

LONDON BOROUGH OF BARNET

BABY CLOWN

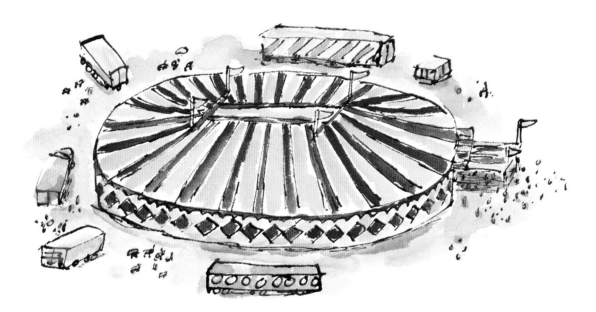

For C. B., the original B. C.
K. L.

To Clara, the youngest performer in the Cordell circus
M. C.

First published 2020 by Walker Books Ltd
87 Vauxhall Walk, London SE11 5HJ

2 4 6 8 10 9 7 5 3 1

Text © 2020 Kara LaReau
Illustrations © 2020 Matthew Cordell

The right of Kara LaReau and Matthew Cordell to be identified as author and illustrator respectively of this
work has been asserted by them in accordance with the Copyright, Designs and Patents Act 1988

This book has been typeset in Filosofia

Printed in China

All rights reserved. No part of this book may be reproduced, transmitted or stored in an information retrieval
system in any form or by any means, graphic, electronic or mechanical, including photocopying,
taping and recording, without prior written permission from the publisher.

British Library Cataloguing in Publication Data:
a catalogue record for this book is available from the British Library

ISBN 978-1-4063-9054-4

www.walker.co.uk

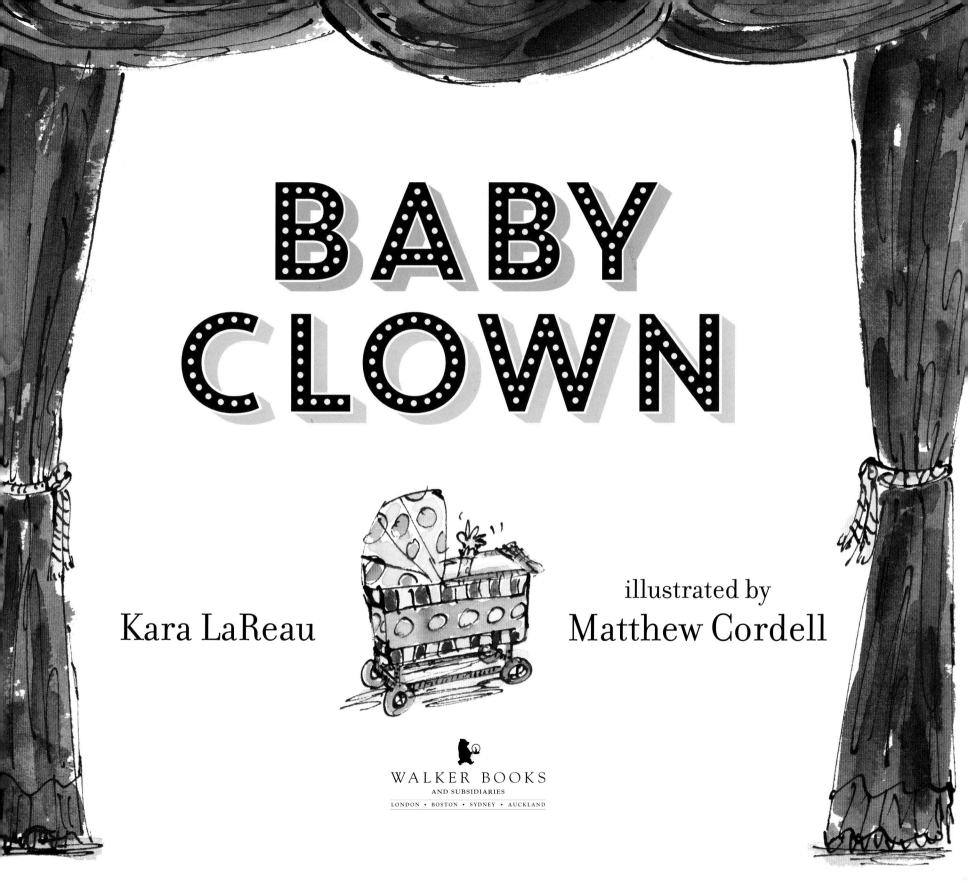

BABY CLOWN

Kara LaReau

illustrated by
Matthew Cordell

WALKER BOOKS
AND SUBSIDIARIES
LONDON • BOSTON • SYDNEY • AUCKLAND

When Boffo and Frieda Clown had a baby,
everyone in the circus was over the moon.
"A STAR is born!" said the big boss, Mr Dingling.
"We'll call him Baby Clown."

There was just one problem. Baby Clown was not a very happy baby.
He cried all the time.

"Somebody'd better cheer up that baby," warned Mr Dingling.
"My clowns do not wear frowns!"

Boffo and Frieda tried everything.

They fed Baby Clown when he was hungry

and burped him when he was windy

and changed his nappy when he was poopy

and rocked him when he was sleepy.
But still, Baby Clown cried.

WAAAAAH!!! WAAAAAH!!! WAAA

The Clowns tried juggling.

They tried driving around in their tiny car.

They tried making their silliest clown faces.
But still, Baby Clown cried.

WAAAAH!!! WAAAH!!!

The Clowns asked for help from the other performers.

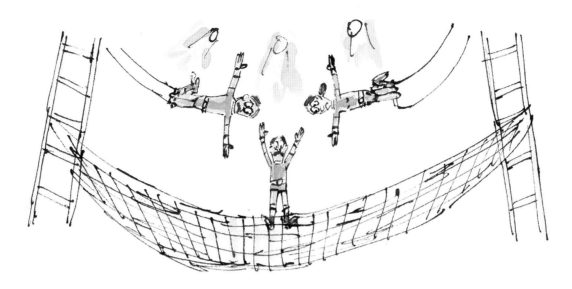

The trapeze artists tried.

Then the animals tried.

Even the tightrope walker tried.

But still, Baby Clown cried.

WAAAAH!!! WAAAH!!! WAAAH!!!!

"Maybe he doesn't want to be a clown," said Boffo.
But when he and Frieda tried to remove Baby Clown's red nose and
jaunty hat and striped pants and big shoes, Baby Clown cried even harder.

WAAAAAH!!! WA

"What is *wrong* with that baby?" asked Mr Dingling. "There is no room
 for crying in my circus!"

"We've tried," said Boffo.

"And we've tried," said Frieda.

"And we've tried, and we've tried, and we've tried," said the other performers.

"Well, keep trying," said Mr Dingling. "The show must go on!"

That night, the circus was sold out. The crowd was thrilled to see the trapeze artists

and the animals on parade and the death-defying tightrope act.

But Baby Clown was not thrilled.

WAAAAH!!! WAA

"Oh, no," said Frieda.

"What should we do?" said Boffo.

"The show must go on," Mr Dingling said.

He walked out to the centre ring and shouted into his megaphone,
"And nooooow … the newest addition to the Dingling Circus …

Everyone in the circus held their breath
as everyone in the audience looked at Baby Clown.

And that's when Baby Clown had a *full-blown meltdown*.

WAAAAH!!!

WAAAAH!!!

WAAAAH!!!

He wasn't a clown anymore, or even a baby.
He was just a big, wide, loud mouth.

But the audience didn't mind at all.

They thought Baby Clown's meltdown was part of the act.

In fact, they clapped louder than they ever had before.
"Hooray!" they cheered. "Hooray for Baby Clown!"

And what did Baby Clown do? For a moment, he stopped crying.
As he looked around at the clapping, cheering crowd, his teary eyes grew wide.

His lip trembled.
His mouth opened.
And then…

"Hee-hee-hee!" Baby Clown giggled, clapping his own hands.
And then he made his very own silly clown face!

Everyone in the circus sighed.

"All he needed was *applause*?" said Boffo.

"Now, *that's* funny," said Frieda.

The Clowns gave their baby a happy (and relieved) hug.

Then the whole Clown family gave the crowd their silliest clown faces,
and the crowd gave them a well-deserved standing ovation.
"Hee-hee-hee!" Baby Clown giggled again.

"Just as I thought," said Mr Dingling.

"A STAR IS BORN!"